WARNING

This book contains sexually explicit scenes and adult language. It may be considered offensive to some readers. This book is for sale to adults ONLY.

* * * * * * * * * * * * * * * * * *

Please store your files wisely where they cannot be accessed by underage readers.

ISBN-13: 978-1987863581
ISBN-10: 1987863585

Other Books by Darla Dunbar:

<u>The Romeo Alpha BBW Paranormal Shifter Romance Series</u>

Amanda Walker thinks that she has a normal and boring life. That is until after her 24th birthday. Everything changes when she meets the man who says he was supposed to be her husband. Denying everything the man says, she fights him every step of the way. But after he kidnaps her, Amanda discovers that there are some things about her family that her parents kept a secret all these years. Among the history of the family she learns secrets she thought only happened in story books. Can Amanda tell the difference between truth and lies or is she this mysterious woman that holds the key to a legacy?

<u>Romeo Alpha Blood Lines Romance Series</u>

Twenty-four years have passed in relative peace for Amanda and Romeo. They've raised five children into adulthood and are thoroughly enjoying their lives as the Alpha King and Queen of the werewolves. At twenty-four, Sarina is just stepping into her powers and will be ripe for mating when her birthday comes in two weeks. What no one knows is the danger that lurks just outside their tight knit community. Romeo has made peace with the other clans and has enjoyed that peace, but it will all come crashing down around him when his oldest daughter comes of age to take a mate.

The Alpha Feud BBW Paranormal Shifter Romance Series

Eliza's life consisted of reporting on boring, crowd-pleasing events, like their country livestock fair. With the arrival of two handsome brothers, the lives of Eliza and her best friend, Melissa, are shaken to the core. For Eliza, the arrival of this new man becomes a test of her relationship with her current boyfriend, who she's been happily living with for over six years. Does Hayden, a complete stranger, really wield the power to make Eliza reconsider her relationship with Andrew?

The Alpha Packed BBW Paranormal Shifter Romance Series

Darlene has led a quiet life since suffering through a terrible break-up. She wants nothing more than to spend her time in front of the TV, away from any sort of trouble. But all that goes down the drain when handsome, rugged and rough Idris comes into her life. He is a werewolf on the lookout for his missing pack leader. Darlene quickly finds herself pulled towards this mysterious man and at the same time finds herself falling deeper and deeper into the world of the supernatural.

The Daemon Paranormal Romance Chronicles

The daemon infighting can only be stopped when a strong leader emerges to calm the different factions. Juno appears to be at the heart of the conflict. Things become complicated when Phoebe and Supay try to negotiate with the siren, Juno. The love triangle among Phoebe, Supay and Apollo become tense when Juno's meddling threatens to destroy any romance that develops.

<u>The Mind Talker Paranormal Romance Series</u>

Ananda finds herself on the run and she's not alone. With help from Jared, a stranger that she just met, the two evade capture by an organization that is intent on hunting her kind. Ananda and Jared are able to read minds. When an unfortunate incident happened involving a disturbed individual that resulted in the death of his schoolmates, the secret organization decided to take action.

Get the latest update on new releases from the author at:

https://darladunbar.com/newsletter/

This book is Part One of "The Leather Satchel Paranormal Romance Series"

Book 1 - Valtina's Redemption

Valtina is stuck in Middle World, unable to pass on to The Afterlife. In order to redeem herself from past deeds done, she must help bring romance back into the world and stop The Dark Side from destroying love in its entirety. Following orders issued by Ladaya and armed with a leather satchel filled with the appropriate tools and weapons, Valtina must bring romance back into the lives of Samantha and Joshua, thereby saving their marriage.

Book 2 - Unfaithful

Amy and Matt's relationship was never meant to be. The evil forces at work are bent on eliminating love on Earth. Couples are being mismatched in order to create chaos. It is Valtina's mission the help Amy find her soul mate and repair the damage that is being caused by the dark forces.

Book 3 - Evil Lust

Henry and Claire are meant to be together. But a succubus has taken over Henry's actions. Under her spell, Henry has succumbed to lusting after Charlotte, the human form that the succubus has assumed. If Claire were to find out, then their marriage will be ruined beyond repair. It is up to Valtina to break the succubus' spell and clear Henry's memory of any guilt that would haunt his love for Claire forever.

Book 4 - Salvaged Soul Mates

The Dark Side is winning. A Mystic has organized the evil monsters to steal every soul on Earth and leave it loveless. It is up to Valtina to do her part to save the human race. Sent by Ladaya back to Earth, Valtina's job is to unite a mismatched couple with their true soul-mates. Sebastian and Claudia were not meant to be married to each other. But a trickster was involved in encouraging the mismatch. Searching through her leather satchel, Valtina found the tools needed to do the job.

Book 5 - Fury of Lust

Valtina's missions are becoming more dangerous and will need the protection of a warrior and emere while out on duty. This time she needs to rid Rachel of a fury and free Sean of his demons. Rachel and Sean are meant to be true lovers but they have been prevented from meeting each other. Valtina must use the arsenal in her leather satchel to ensure that true love follows its course when Rachel and Sean finally meet.

Book 6 - True Lovers

Middle World has been invaded by the wraiths. While the Generals battle the monsters to protect Middle World, Valtina must continue her missions to save love on Earth. The evil forces have brain-washed Penelope and Davis into thinking that their attraction for each other is wrong. Valtina's mission is to clear the way for the couple to see that they were meant for each other and to let true love runs its fateful course.

The Leather Satchel Paranormal Romance Series

Valtina's Redemption

Book One

By Darla Dunbar

Copyright Revelry Publishing 2015

Table of Contents

Chapter One

NOT EVERYONE was given a second chance, especially after failing so many times before. Valtina was among the lucky few who got a real opportunity to redeem themselves. She was a spirit trapped in Middle World: a place filled with souls who have gone astray and were not granted entrance into The Afterlife until they have learned a few lessons and found their place. These were lost souls in a way, and Valtina was most likely just a lifetime away from discovering her true identity. Right now, however, she was summoned by Ladaya to discuss a task that may grant her access to The Afterlife if she can complete it successfully. Valtina waited hopefully for her to arrive.

Ladaya has already perfected her soul. She has earned her place in The Afterlife, but she has also learned what it means to help others, and so she returned regularly to guide souls through their journey and to help them succeed on their own paths. Now, she coalesced out of the gray fog surrounding them. Valtina's face lit up with excitement and a hint of nervousness. Thoughts flooded her mind of the different jobs she may be asked to complete, and she was worried that they may not be things she herself can do. Nevertheless, she held her composure, hopeful that she might be reunited with her family and lovers in The Afterlife.

"Hello, Valtina," Ladaya smiled warmly at her.

"Hello."

"Thank you for agreeing to meet me today… I really need your help. If you can do this successfully, I'll reward you in the fullest. It will be worth it in more ways than one, trust me."

"I'm happy to help, but what exactly do you want me to do?"

"Given the grave matter we are dealing with, I am going to need to leave a lot of the decision making to you. But I'll give you a bit of background information to get you started. As you may have noticed in your last life, the world is on a decline, especially in the area of love. Couples are no longer able to love each other the way that they should. Cheating is becoming a normal thing—many partners are having extramarital affairs and sleeping with multiple women while trying to keep up the appearance that they are 'dedicated' to their wives or girlfriend. Even more couples are only staying together because of lust, and no other attraction towards the other person. They don't love each other and their relationships are meaningless.

"This might not seem like a huge problem at first, but the entire universe is based on love and human compassion. That's something that we can't survive without, and evil is tempting people away from their core values. It won't take long before the world is in tatters and everything will fall apart. Now, this is where you come in."

"I'm going to need you to help breathe life and passion back into relationships that have gone stale and started to fall apart. Over the centuries, I've seen how you are in each life that you have lived. You are dripping with sexual energy and you have had some of the most successful relationships that I've ever seen. I know that you can do this job. I need you to do this for me."

Valtina pondered this for a few moments, doubting whether or not she would be able to successfully do the task expected of her. Even though she may have been able to understand everything in the world, she had always been successful in her love life, in every life. She felt confident with the idea that she won't have to save any lives or stop a bombing or anything complicated like that. She smiled as she realized that this could actually be a fun thing for her and she was practically beaming as she started to speak, "All right, I'll do it. Where should I start?"

"Well, to begin with, there's a couple that we know who are truly meant to be together. Their names are Samantha and Joshua. They recently got married—only 4 years ago. Already, their sex lives are deteriorating. I want you to fix this. They haven't been intimate in months. Although I'm not entirely sure why this is, I know that they both would be interested in trying some light bondage and they'll be much better off with a change of pace."

She smiled more, realizing that she would be in her element throughout this job. "Sounds good… I can do that, no problem."

"For you to use, I want you to take this leather satchel. It contains some of the most important things that will help you work with these couples. I'm also going to give you some basic abilities that will help you read their minds or redirect their thoughts; inspire them though, don't take control."

"Sure thing."

"I believe in you, Valtina. I know that you will save us."

Valtina dissolved into the fog and reappeared in a modest apartment. The room was filled with photographs and cozy-looking furniture. In an armchair, Joshua was sitting on his own while his wife was curled up on the couch at the other side of the living room. Valtina stood there taking in the scene, saddened to see a married couple sitting apart when they would obviously be more comfortable sitting together.

A few moments after Valtina got there, as she continued taking in her surroundings, the man stood up and stretched. He yawned, "Honey, I'm going to bed. Are you coming with me?"

It took a moment for Samantha to answer. She was zoned out, staring blankly at the television. "Oh, no, not right now. I think I'm going to read for a while and take a shower first. Have a good night." As she talked, she leaned forward and opened up a book from the coffee table.

"All right, have a good night. I love you."

She didn't answer; she was already pretending to be absorbed in the words on the page in front of her. Even Joshua knew that she heard but chose to ignore him. Valtina was already starting to worry that this job might be harder than she expected as she watched Joshua walk slowly to the bedroom and Samantha sit on the couch, resolved to making him miserable and prolonging her misery. This brief scene was an obvious representation of the heartache that was here.

It was clear that all Joshua wanted was to be closer to this wife, and that was understandable. After all, who wouldn't? With the abilities that Valtina had, she knew that he had been trying for months to improve things with her, but Samantha wasn't willing to do anything else. She was bored and it was clear that things needed to change.

Valtina understood both sides of the situation. Joshua loved his wife and he wanted to make her happy, but he clearly didn't know how. Samantha still loved her husband, but after doing the exact same thing for so long, it was hard to be passionate about vanilla sex. As she considered this, Valtina decided that she will have to start work first thing in the morning.

In the meantime, she reached into her bag and pulled out a pair of handcuffs, a blindfold, and some candles. That should be enough to get them started, although it will take some more work from Valtina to set Samantha up in a way that she would be willing to give it a shot with Joshua. She placed the items on one of the side tables by the bed.

Chapter Two

In the morning, when Samantha's alarm went off, she knew that Joshua had already started coffee in the kitchen. A wave of frustration flooded her; every kind gesture that her husband made just made it harder for Samantha to be annoyed with him. Even though she couldn't rationalize her annoyance, that didn't change the fact that she was irritated by how nice he always was. She needed something different and she craved something that would excite her. All Joshua ever was, was nice; they've never even had a real argument.

Valtina, reading her mind, realized that even now Samantha was imagining herself chained on the bed. A look of excitement crossed Samantha's face, followed soon by surprise and disbelief, probably at having pictured such a thing. She lay in bed thinking about it a little longer, wondering if that had always been something she fantasized about or if that was something new to her. Eventually she decided that she had been considering it for a while.

As she stretched and started getting out of bed, she muttered, "Maybe I should mention it to Josh…"

She smiled, "Or maybe I should insist on it."

She stood up, getting out of bed and felt the last bit of sleep starting to leave her. For the first time in weeks, she felt the need for physical contact; despite the fact that she hadn't even allowed Joshua to kiss her for the past few days, she wanted him now. Valtina put this desire in her, hoping to push her in the right direction.

Now, she walked toward him at the counter, where he was arranging the breakfast that he made for them. Samantha came up next to him and wrapped her arm around him lightly, leaning against him. He didn't miss a beat and returned the hug, kissing her lightly on the forehead despite his surprise. "Good morning, beautiful."

They ate quietly and barely spoke, though this was not unusual for them. While they ate, Samantha couldn't help but study her husband. There was something incredibly different about him this morning-- thanks to Valtina--and she couldn't quite put her finger on it. Her eyes traveled over his muscles, which she seemed to have never really noticed before. She also noticed that his hair looked disheveled and sexy after his shower, and it fell perfectly around his handsome face. And, although she couldn't quite determine what it was, there was another subtle change in him that kept drawing her to her husband, making her want him more and more.

After a little while, Samantha realized that maybe it was not something so different about Joshua but maybe something different in her. Some of the thoughts she had this morning were surprising and unlike her typical behavior. For the first time in years, she was unable to take her eyes off her husband.

Thoughts traveled through her mind of things that she never would have imagined before. The idea of being held in her husband's strong, muscular arms and having complete control over her… she couldn't help but grow more and more excited. There was something appealing in the images she had of being completely at his mercy. Even though she had never given it any serious thought until now, this kinkier fantasy was something she would love to try and it could be exactly what they needed to spice things up.

Samantha glanced at her watch and realized that she was starting to run late. "I'm going to get going, okay?"

"Sure, have a good day at work. Love you."

"I love you too." She bent down and kissed him, then took her dishes to the sink and grabbed her purse on the way out. As she pulled the door shut behind her, she turned for one last look at her husband. There was a part of her that didn't ever want to look away, and already Valtina's plans were starting to have their effect on her.

Chapter Three

Through the next few hours at work, she had a difficult time concentrating on her job. Her mind constantly wandered off to thoughts of Joshua. By the time she took her lunch break, Samantha has been so distracted that she barely managed to accomplish anything. Rather than waste even more time, Valtina convinced Samantha to take a half day and just leave. Thankfully, it had been a slow day at the office and her boss didn't mind her leaving.

She drove home, still imagining the things that she wanted Joshua to do to her. She stopped at a gas station to fill up her car; while she was waiting there, she called Josh.

He picked up immediately, "Hey, is everything all right?"

"Yeah, umm, everything is fine. I was just kind of wondering if you could come home early. I'm on my way home now; I thought maybe we could… talk."

Instantly, he knew what she meant and sounded just as interested as his wife. They were still connected enough to their marriage to know that they were on the same page and that instant connection was something that wouldn't be changed.

"I'll be home in 10 minutes. Don't start without me."

Samantha's heart was racing as she hung up the phone. She finished pumping gas and went in to pay. She took her time, knowing that if she turned up early she would start to get nervous. Valtina helped to encourage her, making her feel confident and sexy as hell. As long as she didn't show up early and have to spend a few minutes alone waiting for Joshua to show up, there wouldn't be a problem.

While she drove home, she combed her hair and put it back into place. She stopped at a red light and fixed her makeup, sprayed on a tiny bit of perfume, and unbuttoned her blouse a little more. As she pulled into the house, she even decided to slide off her panties and put them in her purse, thinking of how that'll save time later on when things got started.

Joshua's car was already in his spot, and the front door was open as she walked down the hallway to their apartment. She pushed the door open all the way and was disappointed when she was greeted only with an empty room. Josh was nowhere in sight, and the place looked just as it did when she left for work this morning, aside from the clean dishes drying on the rack. Assuming that he was waiting in the bedroom, Samantha walked a little ways inside. All she found was the empty room and a freshly made bed.

She ran her hands through her hair, filled with confusion. She started turning around to take another look at the apartment, searching for him. Before she could turn the full way around however, a large warm hand covered over her mouth. In that instant, a silk blindfold was slipped over her eyes and she could no longer see anything around her.

"Don't make a sound, or else." Joshua's husky and aggressive voice soothed and excited her at the same time. Samantha knew that she was all right, but the anticipation of the much more exciting things soon to follow was already starting to make her wet. For now, she decided to follow his order, even as he started pushing her toward the bed.

As she lay there, she heard him rustling through something in the corner of their room on the table. Valtina realized that she must have placed the items in the right place. Joshua thought that Samantha left them there before work, and he immediately jumped into action to please his wife.

Soon, Joshua returned to the bed and Samantha could hear the clink of metal in his hands. She waited there, with every fiber of her being crying out with desire. She wanted to feel the contact of their skin, the sound of his voice, and the taste of him in her mouth. Anything. All she wanted was him right now, but the blindfold prevented her from knowing what was happening. She was completely cut off and vulnerable, and the idea of this exhilarated her.

She soon realized that the clinking must be a set of handcuffs. The cold metal touched her wrist, enclosing it, and she heard it click into place. In a moment, he dragged her arms up over her head, pulled the chain of the handcuffs around one of the bedposts, and cuffed her other wrist above her as well. She was held in position, even more vulnerable than before. It didn't take more than a minute before she could feel a soft material at her ankle. Her legs were spread wide as he tied her legs to the other bedposts, leaving her exposed.

"You look incredible like this, my dear. How do you feel?"

She didn't answer him, although she desperately wanted to; she refused to break his rules. In all truth though, she was tingling with pleasure. The inability to move thrilled her, and she was enjoying this new experience of having herself exposed in such a way. Even though he had barely touched her and she had almost no stimulation, she was already growing very moist. Valtina had done a great job already: if Samantha was already getting wet just from the excitement and anticipation of what was to come, then it would be even better as Joshua started to really go to work and take advantage of her helplessness.

Joshua's hands started exploring her body, traveling over Samantha's calves and thighs, moving slowly closer to her most sensitive areas with each touch. Quickly, he tore up her skirt, revealing her smooth, bare skin. It was instantly noticeable that she was not wearing any panties underneath the skirt. Her mind flew to the underwear that she had stuffed in her purse and she couldn't help but feel shy, even though this man had seen her completely exposed before. Somehow, this time was entirely different from anything that they had done before.

"Mmm, you were ready for me, weren't you? I love how you've already removed your panties. Now, let's see underneath your shirt…" He unbuttoned her shirt quickly, with one simple tug that Samantha never would have expected from his typically clumsy fingers. It took less than a minute for her to be completely exposed. He unhooked her bra and pulled it aside.

Samantha was completely at her husband's mercy.

"You must really have been horny if you called me at work. I've waited so long for that call… You shouldn't have kept me waiting, Sammy."

She moaned, even though she tried to stop herself. Instantly, she was met with a sharp stinging pain on her left breast as he smacked her. Although he didn't smack her in a particularly rough fashion, there was still some force behind it. He didn't do it to hurt her, and the sensation hardened her nipples, making them more sensitive. In that same moment, Joshua took notice of this and decided to stimulate her nipples further with his fingertips.

In a moment, he climbed onto the bed next to her. She could feel the solid presence at her side, and he placed his hands on her breasts, massaging them roughly. She was already struggling not to squirm with the pleasure. This stimulation felt amazing to her, and he was starting to drive her wild. Even though she loved being bound here on the bed, a small part of her wished that she could get up and show him how pleasurable this whole experience was for her already.

But there was still much more to come, and her body was craving penetration.

"You've been a very bad girl, ignoring me and refusing to let me get close to you. This is your punishment… Since you came to me today, though, you will certainly be rewarded."

Samantha nodded her appreciation, still overly excited at his touch, squirming with the pleasure of each movement. Then, quite suddenly, his fingers left her nipples. She braced herself against the impact, knowing what was coming. Although she feared the pain and cringed away from it, she still craved the sting of his palm on her flesh. Joshua kept her waiting just a moment longer, purposely building her anticipation and craving. Then, he lifted his hand and made contact with her soft pubic mound.

Until that very moment, Samantha had never really appreciated just how sensitive this area could be. Over and over, she enjoyed the sensation of his hand stinging her pussy and inner thighs. With each slap, she felt herself growing wetter and more sensitive. Finally, after about ten strokes, he stopped and let his hand rest on her mound.

Joshua bent down, placing a delicate kiss on her forehead and then again on her lips. "You look beautiful right now, with your pussy and thighs glowing bright red. You are so bound and vulnerable…" She could hear him breathing faster in his excitement. His heart was racing. He bent down lower and started kissing and sucking on her skin in different places.

Eventually, he reached her collar bone. Now, even the slightest touch sent chills through her entire body. She was trembling with excitement and pleasure, and he was panting with anticipation.

"Please…" She didn't mean to speak, and she immediately bit her lip.

"'Please' what?"

"Please Josh, I need it…"

"What do you need babe? I want to hear you say it now."

He knew that she had always been shy. She had always had a hard time saying anything crude or inappropriate, and it became even more difficult when they were being intimate together. Even though it was something that Samantha had always struggled with, it was also something that turned him on immensely. When they first started dating, she made more of an effort to be dirty and say things that would excite him more, but that stopped after a year or two. Valtina stepped in and gave her the motivation to do it now, wanting to see the effect that it would have on Joshua.

Although it was not quite as dirty as Valtina would have expected, it did still seem to have the effect that Josh and Sam were looking for. "I need… I need you inside of me."

"You want my fingers? Tell me what you want."

"No daddy. I'll take your fingers if that's all that you're willing to give… But I want to feel your big cock buried deep inside me."

Josh tensed with excitement. Clearly this was not something Samantha had ever said before. His mouth locked onto her right nipple, biting it gently, teasing it with his teeth and flicking it up and down with his tongue. Samantha lay beneath him, writhing in pleasure and pain. He climbed on top of her, spreading her legs even wider. He stopped for a moment, pausing to bend back down and placed his face between her thighs.

"Mm, babe, you smell even better than usual right now. I can tell how aroused you are." Her labia were swollen and red from the rough slaps earlier. She felt sore and that soreness translated into absolute pleasure as he kissed her there, his tongue on her clit.

She tried to fight the sharp moan that escaped her lips, and she couldn't help but pant slightly from the ecstasy she was experiencing. She was not used to having his tongue down there; oral sex wasn't something that either of them typically engaged in, and so it was a strange sensation to her. Even if it felt unusual, it still felt utterly remarkable and her eyes started rolling back in her head.

Josh continued flicking his tongue up and down, and he soon started using his fingers to spread her pussy lips wide. She started biting her lip, hoping that he would start to use those fingers on her, at least until he started penetrating her with his huge, erect penis. Right now, she needed to feel something deep inside her. She wanted to be filled up, and he wanted nothing more than to be inside her.

After months of not cuddling with one another, they were in desperate need for this pleasure. She wanted him to enjoy it just as much as she already was. Mercifully, he thrust one finger deep inside of her. He knew all the right ways to tantalize her insides. He was driving her inside, and it was more pleasure than she could really handle. She felt herself shaking and trembling at his touch.

"Joshua… Please let me please you. This feels so amazing, I want to return it."

"Trust me, you will. But for now, I want to taste you. You haven't let me in for so long."

Soon, she felt as though she was going to explode at his touch. His fingers stimulated her g-spot, each movement bringing her closer and closer to orgasm. At the same time, he sucked hard on her clit, pleasing her in ways that she never even imagined were possible. From head to toe, all of her nerves were tingling with pleasure. She was so close to climax now, she could hardly contain herself.

"I want you to cum for me, Samantha." It was a command and she was more than happy to obey. In an instant, every muscle in her body was rejoicing at his touch and she was quivering in a puddle of her sweat and juices while he continued to lick, kiss, and suck on her most sensitive areas.

After her orgasm was over, he moved out of the way and allowed her to catch her breath for a little while. She tried to relax and focused on bringing her breathing back down to normal. She was still enjoying the electric waves of power that were emanating through her core. She was surprised when she realized that his hands were at her ankles and he was untying her. This sent her into a fresh wave of confusion; she had expected to stay where she was for a bit longer than this.

"What are you doing?" she asked.

"I've given you your orgasm. Samantha, it's your turn to thank me."

She moaned as he started taking one of the cuffs off her wrist. Rather than completely releasing her, Josh just moved her arms away from the bedpost and cuffed her again, ensuring that her hands were restrained in front of her. She had a little more ability to move now.

"Sit up."

She did as she was told, sitting up and stretching. Until she was able to move, she didn't realize that her arms and legs were sore already, after just a short while of being kept in that position. She moved out of the way as he got into position, lying back down on the bed. He rested with his back against the headboard.

"Now, you're going to suck my dick for a little while. Just until I tell you to… Remember, you are not allowed to use your hands for anything except to help you balance. You will use your lips and tongue for the rest."

"Thank you."

He reached out and grabbed her by the hair, pulling her down to his cock. She looked at his huge, throbbing member and immediately started growing even wetter. Oral was still not something that she typically took part in. She was more than happy to, but now that she was down low and facing him head-on she started to feel shy and unsure of herself.

She started by placing soft, delicate kisses on it, and then began moving her tongue in circles around the head of his cock. He interrupted her.

"Sweetheart, I know you can be nasty. Stop trying to be cute and suck me."

This command fueled her horniness, and she followed the order. Immediately she started sucking on his cock hungrily, moving up and down and preparing to deep throat him. With a little effort, she managed to relax her throat enough to take him in entirely. She couldn't remain there long because she started gagging, but based on his reaction it seemed that she had the right effect. He shuddered pleasantly underneath her.

In response to this, she moaned with his penis still in her mouth, knowing how much he enjoyed the vibrations that this caused. She drew back a little, breathing and blowing cold air onto his soaking wet cock. He was breathing faster and growing even harder underneath each light touch. Samantha spat nastily on his dick and started moving up and down again, feeling him enter her mouth a little deeper with each swallow.

She knew how much he was enjoying this and so she was not surprised when he knotted his hand in her hair and started forcing her to go up and down again. He pushed her face down deeper on his huge length and she started deep throating him over and over again. While he moved her head, she tried to concentrate on the motions that she was making with her tongue and she started to suck harder.

He gave her a break after a little while, so she had a chance to breathe. She was panting and her eyes were watering, but she loved every moment of this. She looked up and they locked eyes. The expression in his eyes turned her on even more.

"Lick my balls," he panted.

She did as she was told and started moving lower to lick his ball sac and suck on his testicles. She placed sloppy kisses and sucked gently on him. They were both enjoying this. While she pleasured his balls, Joshua reached down and started touching himself. Samantha looked into his eyes while she worked with her tongue and he smiled down at her.

"Good… You can stop now." He was still breathing heavily, "I want you to get on top of me. You're going to ride me now."

Joshua knew that she didn't like to ride. Samantha was raised with the idea that sex was something men wanted, and they should have to do the work because of that. Valtina immediately removed this idea from her head; there was no reason for her to refuse to ride. She was immediately more than happy to ride; she was thrilled to do whatever it took to get him inside her.

At first, it was somewhat difficult to get on top of him because her hands were cuffed in an awkward position. Josh reached out and took hold of her arm to help her balance while she straddled him. She could feel his erect cock throbbing between her legs and she ground her wet pussy against it, loving the way that it felt when it hit her clit. He let her continue like this for a moment, while enjoying the sensation of her moistness on his hard cock. Then, he reached down and helped guide him inside her.

The instant that the head of his cock was in her, she was already starting to feel the throbbing pressure. She loved to be filled up like this and he loved the wet tightness of her muscles.

Slowly, she lowered herself onto him, taking every inch of his length inside of her, feeling her tight pussy being stretched open. She didn't like having her hands cuffed in front of her, between her chest and his, so she moved to put her arms around his neck, with her hands behind his head. This let her get closer to him and their chests were pressed together as she started to move up and down.

They were breathing at the same time, panting, gasping, and moaning in pleasure as she started to ride him. She wondered why she didn't like to ride before. It felt much better than their typical missionary position.

He was getting much deeper and every movement stimulated her g-spot. While she rode, he started kissing and sucking on her neck. His hands were on her ass now.

The faster she moved, the better it felt. She raised herself up and slammed herself down against him, loving the way that it felt with more force behind it. He bit her neck and slapped her butt, squeezing her cheeks while she rode. They stayed like this for a while, moving together and panting in pleasure at the same time. It didn't take long, however, for her to approach climax again.

"Joshua… I'm going to… explode."

He grabbed her ass, guiding her movements as he moaned, "So am I."

Josh smacked her ass one more time and kissed her on the mouth, biting her lip hard as she continued to ride. With one more movement, she could feel his cock throbbing inside her, pumping her full of his cum. She immediately exploded, climaxing at the same time while she felt her muscles tensing and pulsing against his member deep inside her. Never before had they felt such pleasure and ecstasy in one moment. This orgasm lasted much longer than usual and she couldn't stop kissing him.

He pulled her closer, holding her tightly while they panted, enjoying their simultaneous orgasms. He bit her lip and squeezed her ass. They were both breathing so heavily and trembling with pleasure that she didn't want this moment to end. Through this, she forced out the words, "I love you, Joshua."

"I love you too."

This was definitely the best day of their marriage that they've had in a long time. Samantha didn't want to stop touching him or looking at him. Now that their sex lives had improved, Valtina knew that something more was going to change between them. In this moment, Samantha was so happy with Joshua that she couldn't even remember why she was upset in the first place and he didn't want to give the matter another thought ever again. This moment was completely perfect and it belonged entirely to them.

Valtina watched them panting and clutching at each other, trembling from head to toe. It made her feel good to know that she had helped them. She thought that she had managed to do her job now, and she had brought a little passion back into their love lives.

"Maybe now," she thought, "I can get some peace."

As she decided this, the mist started rolling in over her and she was immediately transported back to Middle World. Ladaya was there, waiting for her with a huge smile on her face. "You did incredibly well, Valtina. Already, there is a little more light in the world. Things will get better between them and the universe will be a little happier now because of you. I'm so proud... I didn't expect you to succeed so quickly. Truthfully, I tried to help them a few times and

I made little progress over weeks of time, let alone just two days."

Valtina was happy to hear that, "Does that mean that I can go now? I can have my Afterlife and my peace now?"

Ladaya's smile faltered for a moment, "What do you mean?"

"I did the job that you asked of me," Valtina fumed, already angry. "I apparently did it better than even you could. Ladaya, you promised that I would 'be rewarded in The Afterlife' if I did this."

She looked puzzled for a moment before she realized what Valtina was saying. "Oh, Valtina, yes you will receive your reward when you finish your job… You helped one couple achieve the happiness and passion that they needed in their lives, but there are many more couples who need help too. Joshua and Samantha were not the only ones in need of your help. Even though there is more love in the universe now because of that couple, there are still many other people who are cheating and lusting after one another without forming any valuable relationships. There is still so much left for us to do."

With each word Ladaya spoke, Valtina's heart sunk a little more as she realized the true magnitude of this task. She was no longer quite so sure that she would be able to do this job after all. One couple might have been easy, but she couldn't imagine that they will all be so simple.

-To be continued in Book 2-

If you enjoyed this title, I would appreciate your leaving a review of the book. Good reviews encourage an author to write as well as help books to sell. Good reviews can be just a few short sentences describing what you liked about the book without having a spoiler. If you could spend 30 seconds writing a review, I would appreciate it: you can review this title right now at your favorite retailer.

Here is a preview of the **next story** you may enjoy:

Unfaithful - The Leather Satchel Paranormal Romance Series, Book 2

EVEN THOUGH Valtina had had a great time helping Joshua and Samantha, she was having a hard time accepting the fact that her job was not yet over. After all, it was very difficult to go from thinking she was on her way to The Afterlife as a reward for finishing her job to the realization that she'd only just barely completed the first task in a list of many. She stood there, trying to come to terms with the idea that she still had a long way to go.

"So… am I really the only one who can do this job? Am I the only person you have?"

"Valtina, there are many people who can help me work with these couples, but you are by far the best at what you do. Don't think that you are the only soul at work right now. Currently, I have at least a dozen others on Earth completing their own missions. That is not your concern right now. The better you help each of these couples, the more the universe will improve and the sooner you can continue on to The Afterlife. For now, though, I need your help."

Valtina paused for a moment, wondering if she really wanted to ask her next question. She did anyway, saying, "Okay Ladaya… But just how many people are we talking about? How many more couples do I have to help along?"

"Right now, I am not sure. The Dark Side is currently working against us and they are gaining power quickly. Every day, they bring more and more people over to their side. Now, it is a matter of how many of these people we can save. We need to bring as many souls back to the light as possible, otherwise we will lose this battle forever."

Clearly, this was a very serious task. This put a great deal of pressure on Valtina and the other souls at work. "I'm going to give you some of the hardest tasks, because I know that you will be able to complete them. I will not ever give you any jobs that I don't think that you can complete. In love, you are the best person that we have."

Ladaya smiled kindly at Valtina, trying desperately to convince her. For a few minutes, Valtina mulled over her options, or at least tried to. It didn't take her long to realize that she had only one other option. However, she didn't want to be reincarnated again. After living countless lives in various bodies and time periods and situations, she was tired of all of the work and monotony. She sighed heavily, "Alright Ladaya, where do you want me to go next?"

"Next, I have a couple that is the perfect example of what will become of the world if The Dark Side wins. They feed off of misery, despair and lust. Each couple that they drag over is living in a great deal of unhappiness. Matt and Amy are the next couple that you will work with. They have been together since they were teenagers, when Matt got Amy pregnant right before their high school graduation. Although Amy never gave birth, they had already moved in together and have been living with each other ever since."

"Matt rarely gives Amy a second thought at this point. He has basically forgotten all about her, and she is completely alone. Right now, she is almost entirely dependent on Matt's income, and she can't move back in with her parents. She is trapped where she is, and she feels that she has no choice but to stay with Matt and watch as he sleeps with numerous girls on the side. You need to help get her out of there."

"Unfortunately, I do not believe that there is any hope for Matt. He has been taken too far over and he lives in lust every day. There is very little that can be done for him at this point, although we may be able to help him further down the road. For now though, we will have to focus on getting Amy to a better place… I have been keeping an eye on the situation for some time now, trying to determine what the best option would be for her. I want you to bring her to Kyle, a man who lives in the same apartment building. Do what you can for her. Here is your leather satchel. I've added a few items for your quest. Take care."

Ladaya was much more abrupt in this encounter, trying to get rid of Valtina faster so that she didn't have any time to protest or ask questions. The less time she had to think over the mission, the better. So, as soon as she stopped speaking, Ladaya transported Valtina to Amy and Matt's apartment building.

Valtina traveled through space and time, watching the fog and mist disperse as she reached her destination. In the matter of only a few seconds, she had left Middle

World and returned to Earth yet again. This time, she appeared in a dark alley in a neighborhood that must have been a lower class residential area. The worn brick of the apartment building next to her didn't seem trustworthy, and Valtina walked out from the alley toward the main road.

As she turned the corner, she saw a young man getting out of his car and jogging around the front of it. As he turned, he lost his balance and started to fall. After barely catching himself, he started laughing along with the girl in the passenger seat. They were both smiling as he opened the door for her and reached his hand out as an offering. She took it saying, "Thanks for the ride, Matt."

For a moment, Valtina was confused. She had automatically assumed that this man and woman were Matt and Amy, though it appeared she was only half correct. Seeing movement out of the corner of her eye, she saw a woman standing in an upstairs window, watching the scene taking place below. The sadness on her face was contagious and Valtina instantly sympathized with her. She left the window, turning away from her boyfriend. This was probably a smart choice because Matt leaned in and kissed the young woman as he pulled her from his car.

"Anytime, baby doll. You sure you don't want me to drive you the other block back to your apartment? Maybe I could stay for a while."

"Matt, I'm sure that your girlfriend is waiting for you already. You don't need to make me feel even guiltier!"

"She doesn't mind. It's not like we have any plans for tonight anyway."

"No Matt, thanks for the offer but I'll be fine walking… it's just a little bit further anyway." She turned and waved over her shoulder, walking away from him. She swayed her hips when she walked and he couldn't take his eyes off her ass.

"Hate to see you go, but love to watch you leave!" he called after her. Then he went inside, up the stairs to his apartment. Valtina followed close behind, despite her disgust at being so near him.

When they entered the apartment, it was easy to see that they didn't have a lot of money. It seemed most of this apartment was filled with cheap DIY furniture and cheap decorations. Although it was obvious that there wasn't a large budget for this home, it was also easy to see that a great deal of attention and consideration went into every aspect of the place. Valtina could feel Amy's energy coming from every direction. She was waiting on a bar stool at the kitchen counter as Valtina and Matt entered.

"Hey babe. How was work?"

"It was fine. Is dinner ready?" He walked over without glancing at her, picked up the plate of food that was set out for him, and took it to a recliner. He sat down, flipped on the TV, and took a bite of the food.

He was served chicken and rice, and she automatically walked over to take out a cold beer from the refrigerator.

"Chicken's cold," he said gruffly.

"Sorry, I had it ready but you're a little later coming home than you usually are."

"Well, you can heat it up again."

She put the beer down on the counter, bowed her head, and took the plate. As she was doing this, Valtina removed a clear, colorless potion from the leather satchel and poured a few drops in the beer. After placing the plate in the microwave oven, Amy handed Matt the beer and returned to the kitchen. In a few minutes, Amy returned to Matt to serve the reheated chicken. She walked in a depressed manner, as though she was completely terrified of the man that she lived with. As she handed him the plate of food, she watched expectantly, waiting to see if he enjoyed it more this time around.

If you enjoyed this sample then look for **Unfaithful - The Leather Satchel Paranormal Romance Series, Book 2.**

Here is a preview of **another story** you may enjoy:

The Awakening: The Daemon Paranormal Romance Chronicles, Book 1

THE LAST customer of the day was slowly leaving. Phoebe reached down to pet her dog, Ace, and moved to close up shop. Since graduating high school, she had worked in fairs across the country as a fortune teller, saving money. She did not know why, but when she touched somebody's hand, she could read their thoughts. Although she could not divine their future, she could make educated guesses that were enough to bring customers back. After saving enough money, she had finally opened up her own shop.

Removing the scarf from around her hair, Phoebe let her red curls cascade along her shoulders. Ace sniffed at some of his dog food while she reached over to grab her purse. Before she could close up, a knock at the door surprised her. In front of the door, she saw one of the most gorgeous men she had ever laid eyes on. Curious, she opened the door and let him in.

"Hello! How can I help you, Mr...?" She paused and waited for him to respond.

"My name is Apollo Mikos. Pleasure to meet you, Phoebe Williams." The blonde-haired man reached for her hand and shook it. Instantly, a vision arose before her eyes of Apollo and her rolling around in bed sheets. Waves crashed outside the window—a storm was brewing. As the vision of Apollo entered her body forcefully, Phoebe pulled her hand back. The vision went away, but it left a slight blush on Phoebe's cheeks. Reading the minds of other people was occasionally embarrassing and often felt like a major invasion of privacy. Still, she found herself wishing that she could have held his hand a little longer to see where these thoughts took her.

Motioning toward the table and chairs reserved for clients, she asked if he wanted to sit down. Apollo just shook his head.

"I need your help with something, but not like that." He shrugged his shoulders. Tall and well-built, Apollo had blue eyes and chiseled features. He wore a dark black suit that made all of his muscles ripple beneath the fabric.

Confused, Phoebe looked over at him. "What do you mean?"

Sighing, Apollo looked into her eyes. "You will probably want to sit down for this." Still uncertain, Phoebe sat down and waited for him to speak again.

Gazing out the window, Apollo framed his thoughts. "I know your mother, Rhea. I also know what you really are and I need your help."

Phoebe was aghast. "What do you mean? I don't have a mother. I grew up in foster care after my mother left me there when I was two."

If you enjoyed this sample then look for **The Awakening: The Daemon Paranormal Romance Chronicles, Book 1.**

Here is a preview of **another story** you may enjoy:

Secrets Revealed: Obsessed Bounty Hunter New Adult Romance Series, Book 1 by Carla Coxwell

JACQUI SCHNEIDER awoke with a sudden start, the unfamiliarity of her surroundings sending waves of panic sweeping all through her body. Her head whipped frantically from side to side as her eyes swept across the shadowy interior.

She could see the white sheer curtain drawn across the glass window. The sky outside the window had a purplish hue, indicating the first blush of dawn. A console table just below the window held a tray with a thermos bottle and a cup and saucer set neatly stacked beside it. A beige telephone and a digital clock with the time displayed as 4:27 a.m. rested on the other side of the console table. She recognized her clothes as they lay strewn on the floor. Her high-heeled shoes and purse lay in a pile near the door.

She was in a hotel room. As awareness took over, Jacqui was glad her sudden movement did not disturb the sleeping form beside her. She glanced at the figure snoring softly and saw his hand reach out for her. He stirred, breathing deeply, and then resumed his sleep. Jacqui hoped he would not notice the empty space beside him as she tiptoed silently out of bed and gathered her clothes from the floor.

Jacqui wanted to leave the hotel before the man woke up. Things were less complicated that way. She couldn't even remember his name. Was it John… or Jack… or Jim…?

Jacqui didn't really care. It was strictly sexual. She had no intention of ever seeing him again. He was just a random guy she had picked up in the hotel bar last night. The guys were always the same. Non-threatening, married, from out of town, and only out to have a good time. A few made a play of removing their wedding rings. But Jacqui could always spot the telltale lighter skin tone where the ring used to be.

This suited Jacqui just fine. It wasn't a good idea to hook up with someone local. She always made sure the guy was at the hotel for a convention, or just an overnight stay. She usually spotted them because of the name tag pinned over their breast pocket. She'd sit in the bar with her drink, until someone struck up a conversation or offered her a drink.

Jacqui was very hard not to notice. She was tall and lithe and had full breasts, milky white skin, and a nice round ass. She had sparkling green eyes, high cheekbones and luscious lips, topped by chestnut brown hair that fell softly to her shoulders; she attracted instant attention.

And this guy…Jim…Jacqui suddenly remembered, was no different. He made a beeline for her as soon as he spotted her at the bar.

"Hi, my name's Jim… I hope you don't mind the intrusion…" Jacqui remembered him saying. "But it looks like your glass needs a refill."

Jacqui gave him a smile. It was the standard pickup line. He didn't know she already pegged him through the glass mirrors lining the liquor cabinet of the bar. He was going to be "it" for tonight.

"Are you staying in this hotel?" Jim asked, signaling the bartender for another shot of brandy for her.

"No…" Jacqui answered.

"Are you waiting for someone…?" Jim asked.

Jacqui could read the expectant look in his eyes, and this was usually her cue. If she didn't like what she saw or if she had second thoughts about her safety, she'd say… "Yes, I'm just waiting for my boyfriend to pick me up…" Or offer some other lame excuse.

But she had liked what she saw. Jim was tall, good-looking and neatly dressed. And he had a ring on his finger.

"No…" Jacqui answered and gave him a flirty smile. "My name is Nina…" she added.

Yes, she would be a horny Nina tonight, or Glenna, or Linda. It didn't really matter. She just wanted to get laid. And tonight, Jim was it.

Jacqui could predict how the next hour would play out. Jim will tell her his life story as he kept filling up her glass hoping to get her drunk enough so she would be pliant when he made his move. The thought almost made Jacqui laugh. The poor guy didn't know that was exactly her plan.

"You've hardly told me anything about yourself, Nina…" Jim complained playfully, as his hand dropped down to her knee.

"There's really nothing to tell…I'm just a girl hoping to get lucky tonight…" Jacqui whispered seductively in his ear.

His hand moved a little further up her skirt as Jacqui opened her legs a little wider to allow him to feel her crotch through her sheer stockings.

Jim's eyes opened wide in surprise as he felt the heat emanating through the silk.

"Why don't we finish this conversation upstairs in my room?" Jim asked.

Jacqui nodded her head in reply as her bosom heaved in anticipation. This was the reason she was here tonight. This guy, Jim, would make her forget even for just a few hours, those thoughts and images that constantly lurked in her psyche, tormenting her. When they came uninvited, Jacqui knew what would make her forget. Sex.

Jacqui sashayed her way out of the bar ahead of him. She wanted him to see her firm ass, tapered waist, and long slim legs. It was hard to ignore the looks from other men that followed her and this aroused her even more. She made her way out and straight into the banks of elevators.

Jim could hardly contain his excitement. His erection was bulging through his pants.

As soon as the bedroom door closed behind them, Jacqui dropped down on her knees and unzipped his pants. She grabbed hold of his cock. She spit down on it as her hands feverishly stroked it. Jim was hardly out of his pants before Jacqui had him inside her mouth.

Jim threw back his head in arousal. He was stunned at the ferocity with which Jacqui moved her head back and forth, her saliva leaving his shaft red and glistening. Jacqui toyed with the head of his cock and tasted the sweet dew that signaled that he would cum prematurely if she didn't slow down.

And Jim didn't want to cum just yet. He had plans of sucking and tasting every inch of her. He would fuck her hard, until the tension building inside his body became unbearable, and then he would blow his load in her mouth.

He pulled her up and began to unhook her bra. Jacqui's face was wild with anticipation as she shimmied out of her clothes and stockings. A slight sweat broke out in her armpits. Her boobs swelled as Jim groped one breast with his hand and twirled his thumb and forefinger around the sensitive nipple. Using his mouth, he sucked on the other nipple. Jacqui arched her back in pleasure as waves of ice and fire shot straight through to her groin.

Jim continued sucking her breast and nibbling her nipple with his teeth. His other hand traveled down her flat stomach. He stopped just below her mound, feeling the coarse pubes that covered her vagina. Using his fingers to separate the lips, he caressed her clit and discovered just how wet and aroused she was. Jim stroked her clit repeatedly. He slid in another finger, adding pressure with every stroke. He could feel the inner muscles of her vagina tightening each time his hand brushed against her swollen clitoris. Jacqui closed her eyes and moaned her pleasure. Getting fingered felt really good.

But Jacqui knew she wanted more than his fingers. Pulling him along, she lay back against the bed and opened her thighs. Her pussy was slick with her own juice.

"Do you like what you see?" she whispered up at him as Jim nodded.

"Eat me. Show me what your tongue can do…" she whispered huskily as she caressed herself to arouse him.

Jacqui grabbed her knees and spread her legs even wider for him, leaning her head back against the pillow. Her invitation was obvious, insistent.

Jim scrambled up the bed, his erect penis bouncing with the movement. Then he knelt down between her legs, enthralled with the red-hot pussy before him. He lowered his head as his hands separated the lips of her vagina, exposing the engorged clit. He flicked his tongue against it as Jacqui's body heaved with pleasure. He flicked repeatedly; mesmerized by the guttural sounds emanating from Jacqui's mouth each time his rough tongue made contact with the sensitive skin.

She began to moan as he went faster and faster until finally she couldn't take it anymore. She wanted to feel his cock inside her.

Jim positioned himself on top of her. He used his elbows to steady himself as his cock searched for her vagina's opening. Jacqui savored the feeling of the velvety skin of his cock rubbing against the slick wetness of her clit. Jim rammed himself inside her. And then he drew back until the head of his cock was barely past the opening of her vaginal wall. Then he rammed into her once again, filling her completely.

If you enjoyed this sample then look for **Secrets Revealed: Obsessed Bounty Hunter New Adult Romance Series, Book 1 by Carla Coxwell**.

Other Books by Darla Dunbar

- The Romeo Alpha BBW Paranormal Shifter Romance Series

- Romeo Alpha Blood Lines Romance Series

- The Alpha Feud BBW Paranormal Shifter Romance Series

- The Alpha Packed BBW Paranormal Shifter Romance Series

- The Daemon Paranormal Romance Chronicles

- The Mind Talker Paranormal Romance Series

Get the latest update on new releases from the author at:

https://darladunbar.com/newsletter/

About the Author - Darla Dunbar

Darla has been interested in paranormal romance since she was a teenager in high school. It was then that she discovered she could fulfill her fantasies through her writing.

Observing people and human behavior in the area of romance has always been one of her favorite pastimes. Combining that with an overactive imagination is a sure fire way of coming up with interesting themes.

Connect with Darla Dunbar

I really appreciate you reading my book! Here are my social media coordinates:

Friend me on Facebook:
https://www.facebook.com/darladunbar/

Follow me on Twitter: https://twitter.com/DarlDunbar

Check me out on Goodreads:
https://www.goodreads.com/author/show/8425857.Darl
a_Dunbar

Subscribe to my newsletter:
https://darladunbar.com/newsletter/

Visit my website: https://darladunbar.com/

www.ingramcontent.com/pod-product-compliance
Lightning Source LLC
Chambersburg PA
CBHW031631200726

48288CB00019B/1386